Daisy Dawson

Daisy Dawson

Steve Voake

illustrated by Jessica Meserve

WALKER
BOOKS

First published 2007 by Walker Books Ltd
87 Vauxhall Walk, London SE11 5HJ

8 10 9

Text © 2007 Steve Voake
Illustrations © 2007 Jessica Meserve

This book has been typeset in StempelSchneidler

Printed and bound in Great Britain by Clays Ltd, St Ives plc

British Library Cataloguing in Publication Data:
a catalogue record for this book is available from the British Library

ISBN 978-1-4063-0080-2

www.walkerbooks.co.uk

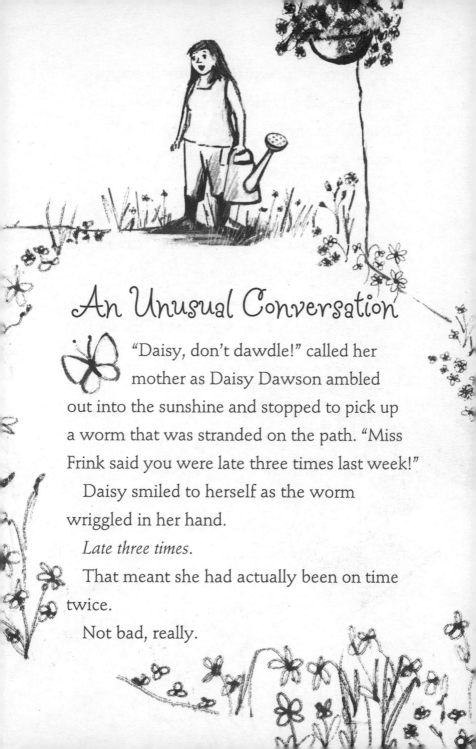

An Unusual Conversation

"Daisy, don't dawdle!" called her mother as Daisy Dawson ambled out into the sunshine and stopped to pick up a worm that was stranded on the path. "Miss Frink said you were late three times last week!"

Daisy smiled to herself as the worm wriggled in her hand.

Late three times.

That meant she had actually been on time twice.

Not bad, really.

She tipped the worm into the flowerbed and watched it burrow through the crumbly earth. Then she stood up, hitched her satchel over her shoulder and skipped down the garden path.

"Don't worry, Mum," she said, dusting her hands together and swinging around the gatepost. "Daisy Dawson is on her way!"

The day was warm and the sky was china blue. Bees buzzed amongst the foxgloves and Daisy wandered down the lane, humming a little tune to herself.

Suddenly, from the corner of her eye, she caught sight of a beautiful yellow butterfly stuck in a spider's web. As she crouched down to take a closer look, a black spider emerged from beneath a leaf and began crawling across the web towards it.

"Oh no you don't!" said Daisy, cupping her hand protectively around the struggling insect. As the spider scuttled back to its hiding place, she scooped the butterfly out of the web and carefully pulled some sticky strands from its wings.

"There you go," she said. "Back in the world again."

Then she smiled and opened her palms towards the sky.

The butterfly was still for a few moments. Then, very slowly, it spread its wings and fluttered gracefully up into the air. Daisy shielded her eyes against the sun and blinked as the butterfly swooped low past her face, brushing her cheek gently with the tip of its wing. Then it rose once more into the warm air and flew high into the treetops, growing smaller and smaller until finally it was lost from sight.

As Daisy watched it fly away, her cheek began to tingle as though something was sparkling beneath her skin. She touched a hand to her face and a delicious warm feeling fizzed along her fingers,

tumbling
like a wave through her
whole body until it reached all the way
down to the tips of her toes.

"How very strange," she whispered.

Just then, somewhere among the white
blossoms of an apple tree, a blackbird began
to sing. Its sweet music floated down
through the summer sky and, to her
astonishment, Daisy realized that she could
understand exactly what it was singing
about. The notes spun softly around her like
strands of silk, weaving a song about clouds
and apples, sunshine and stars.

Daisy gasped in surprise and shook her
head.

"Now don't be *silly*, Daisy," she told
herself. "Pull yourself together. Birds can't
talk."

It was then that she remembered where
she was supposed to be. Only yesterday,

Miss Frink had told her not to be late again.

Pulling up her satchel, she twirled around and wandered slowly on towards school. Across the meadow she could see the white mare tugging at tufts of grass in the shade of the beech tree. Daisy leant on the gate and peered into the shadows of the tumble-down barn, trying to see if the old stray dog was anywhere about. She liked to share a bit of her lunch with him on the way to school. Ham sandwiches were his favourite, and she had made an extra one just in case.

"Rover?" she called, opening up her lunchbox. "Rover, come and see what I've got for you!"

A large, grumpy-looking bloodhound stuck its head through a hole in the bricks, blinking and sneezing in the bright sunlight.

Its fur was the colour of sandstone and its serious brown eyes stared out from folds of baggy skin that hung down around its face. As it padded towards her, its long floppy ears swung back and forth, flapping up dust from the dry ground.

When it reached the gate, it stopped and looked at her expectantly.

"Good morning," it said in a deep, gravelly voice. "What's on the menu today, then?"

Daisy was so shocked that she dropped her lunchbox and put a hand up to her mouth.

This cannot be happening, she thought. She shut her eyes tightly for a moment or two, then opened them again.

The dog was still there, looking straight at her.

"I–I–I beg your pardon," Daisy said uncertainly, still unable to believe her ears, "but did you say something to me?"

"Of course," replied the dog. "It would have been rude not to." He paused for a moment as if deep in thought, then said slowly, "Wait a minute … do you actually understand what I'm saying to you?"

"Yes," replied Daisy. "I think I do."

The dog made a noise somewhere between a bark and a laugh.

"This," he said, "is amazing!"

"But you understand me as well," said

14

Daisy. "So that's pretty amazing too."

The dog cocked his head to one side.

"Dogs always understand what humans say," he replied.

"No they don't," said Daisy. "Take my Auntie Kath's dog. He never does anything she tells him."

The dog's brow crinkled like a little ploughed field.

"That doesn't mean he doesn't *understand* her," he said. "He probably just doesn't want to do it."

"Oh," said Daisy thoughtfully, "I see what you mean."

"There you go then," said the dog.

There was silence for a moment while the two of them thought about this. Then the dog said, "My name's not Rover, by the way. It's Boom." Seeing the puzzled look on Daisy's face he added, "I was born on fireworks night, you see."

"Really?" Daisy smiled. "That must have been a bit of a shock for you."

"It was rather," agreed Boom. "The first thing I saw when I opened my eyes was a thousand rockets exploding above me. Huge blazing stars of red, green, orange and gold. My mother said it was the whole world celebrating my birthday."

Daisy heard the sadness in Boom's voice and guessed he probably didn't see his mother any more.

"Boom's a lovely name," she said. "It suits you."

"Thank you," said Boom. "What about you? Do you have a name?"

"Two actually," said Daisy. "I'm Daisy Dawson."

"Well, Daisy Dawson," said Boom. "I'm pleased to make your acquaintance at last."

"Likewise," said Daisy, and stuck her arm through the gate.

Boom put his soft paw into her hand. As Daisy shook it he asked, "Am I the first dog you've ever spoken to?"

"Not exactly," said Daisy. "I mean, I've spoken to lots of dogs before. But you're the first one who's ever replied."

Boom chuckled. "Well fancy that," he said. Then he licked his lips and peered longingly through the gate at Daisy's fallen lunchbox.

"I don't suppose you've got any spare bits and pieces in there?"

"Of course," said Daisy, picking it up. "Actually, I've brought along your favourite."

Boom raised an eyebrow.

"Not *ham*?" he asked.

"Honey roasted," said Daisy, producing a sandwich with a flourish. "Extra thick."

"You," said Boom, "are an angel from heaven."

Daisy giggled. "Tell that to Miss Frink."

Then she looked at her watch and remembered.

"Oh my goodness," she exclaimed, "I'm going to be late for school!"

"Is that bad?" asked Boom through a mouthful of sandwich.

"Miss Frink thinks so," said Daisy.
She turned to go, then looked
back over her shoulder and waved.
"Nice talking to you, Boom," she
called. "See you again soon."

Then, hitching up her
satchel, she ran down
the dusty lane towards
the gates of Nettlegreen
Primary School.

Cheesy Cheddars

"What was it this time?" asked Miss Frink as Daisy tiptoed into the classroom and mouthed "Sorry I'm late" over the top of Marty Johnson's head. "A tornado perhaps? An avalanche? An earthquake in the lane?"

As the rest of the class tittered into their reading books, Daisy shook her head and slid into her seat. "No, Miss Frink," she said. "It was none of those things."

"Really?" replied the teacher icily. "Well, Daisy, you do surprise me."

Daisy took out her pink pencil case and hooked her satchel over the back of her chair, hoping she might get off lightly this time. But Miss Frink was obviously in the mood for some entertainment.

"Perhaps, then, Miss Dawson, you would like to tell us all exactly why you *are* late again today."

Daisy hesitated. She was an honest girl and it was not in her nature to tell a lie. But she realized that "I've been talking to a dog" was unlikely to go down well with Miss Frink. So she said, "I'm afraid I completely forgot what the time was, Miss Frink."

Which was true, of course. It just left out the interesting bits.

"*Again?*" said Miss Frink.

"Sorry," said Daisy. "I'll try to be on time tomorrow."

"Trying is not good enough," said Miss Frink. "You *will* be on time tomorrow." She snapped the register shut and peered at Daisy over the top of her spectacles. "*Won't* you, Daisy?"

"Yes, Miss Frink," said Daisy. "I promise."

At that moment, Bobby Mitchell fell backwards off his chair and everyone was told to Stop Laughing because it Wasn't Funny and he Could Have Been Killed.

The long, hot morning wore on.

Daisy was soon so busy trying to work out whether 121 ÷ 7 had a remainder (and if so what to do with it) that she quite forgot about her strange conversation with Boom. She had just discovered that the remainder was 2 when she heard a small, squeaky voice say:

"Oh, *wow*. Cheesy Cheddars!"

Daisy looked around to see if anyone else had heard it, but Miss Frink was in the corner explaining Hundreds, Tens and Units to Orange Group, and the rest of the class had their heads down over their maths books.

"I *love* Cheesy Cheddars."

"Hang on, Burb – don't eat 'em all! I'm coming over!"

Glancing into the corridor, Daisy saw a small gerbil scampering beneath the row of coats. It stopped for a second, sniffed the air and then disappeared into a lunchbox that had fallen open on the floor. There was the sound of giggling, followed by crunching noises.

"These are great, aren't they?" said a little voice happily.

"Cheesy Cheddars are my number one favourite," said the other voice. "They taste like the sun just blew up in your mouth."

"*Bam!*" exclaimed the first voice. "Deeelicious!" This was followed by a lot more giggling.

Daisy suddenly remembered that Bobby Mitchell had been playing with the class gerbils – Burble and Furball – earlier that morning. She looked anxiously across at the glass tank full of straw and sawdust and noticed that the top had not been put back

25

on properly. A half-chewed cardboard toilet-roll tube was pushed up against the side of the tank.

Burble and Furball were nowhere to be seen.

Uh-oh, thought Daisy.

Placing her pencil neatly along the crease of her maths book, she thrust her hand up into the air.

"I don't care who started it," Miss Frink was saying to Wayne Bishop. "I'm telling you to stop it Right Now!"

Daisy coughed politely.

"Excuse me," she said.

"Yes, Daisy?" said Miss Frink crossly. "What is it?"

"We haven't taken the register up to the office yet." Daisy smiled her biggest, most helpful smile. "Shall I take it up for you?"

Miss Frink frowned.

"Have you finished your maths yet?"

Daisy looked down at her book.

"Almost," she said. "I'm onto the problems now."

You can say that again, she thought to herself.

"Well," said Miss Frink, softening a little, "that would be very helpful, Daisy. But don't be long. And don't dawdle!"

"I won't," said Daisy, picking up the register from Miss Frink's desk.

She closed the classroom door behind her and stood next to the coats, listening carefully.

"What's your favourite?" asked a small voice. "Sunflower seeds or sandwiches?"

"Dunno," replied another little voice. "I've never had a sandwich." There was a pause. "When have you ever had a sandwich?"

"Well," said the first voice, sounding as though its mouth was full of something, "actually, I'm having one *right now!*"

This was followed by a joyful cry of "Oh, it's a *cheesy* sandwich!" and the sound of little voices giggling with their mouths full.

Daisy crouched down next to the coats.

"Excuse me," she said, "but I think that's someone else's lunch you're eating."

The giggling stopped.

"Did you hear that?" a voice whispered.

"Yes, I did," whispered the other. "Was she talking to us?"

"Don't be daft," said the first voice. "Since when have kids been able to talk to gerbils?"

"Actually, I *am* talking to you," announced Daisy. "And what's more, I know you can hear me."

There was a spluttering noise and the sound of cheesy breadcrumbs being sprayed around the lunchbox. Then a furry little face poked out from under the plastic cover. When it saw Daisy it whipped back inside.

"It's a girl!" it squeaked. "And she *is* talking to us!"

"Pull the other one," said the first voice, "it's got bells on."

"If you don't believe me, take a look for yourself. Go on!"

Another tiny face appeared and stared at Daisy, its shiny brown eyes widening with surprise. Then it shot back inside and banged its head on the lid.

"*Ow–chee!*"

"See? Told you."

"Listen," said Daisy patiently. "I'm not

going to hurt you. I just want a word with you, that's all."

There was a rustling sound and the two gerbils popped their heads out of the lunchbox.

"You're a talking girl!" said one. Daisy recognized him as Furball by the little white patch on his nose. "How amazing is that?"

"Not as amazing as my first ever cheesy sandwich," said Burble. She slid back into the lunchbox and let out a tiny burp. "Oopsy, beg pardon."

"You really shouldn't be out here," said Daisy. "Miss Frink will be very upset if she finds out you've run away."

"Well," replied Burble, "in that case she should give us cheesy sandwiches, shouldn't she?"

"Cheese sandwiches aren't proper food for gerbils," said Daisy. "If you had them all the time you'd probably get ill."

"It'd be worth it," said Furball. "They're *gorgeous*!"

"Listen," said Daisy, trying to get the conversation back on track. "I really think you should go back to your tank now."

"Don't want to," said Furball. "Food's boring and it's got sawdust in it."

"That's 'cos you keep chucking it on the floor," said Burble. "If you ate it out of the dish, there'd be no problem."

"Ooh, hark at her," said Furball, putting on a posh voice. *"'That's because you keep chucking it on the floor...'"* I chuck it on the floor because it's so *boring*. I want Cheesy Cheddars, thank you very much."

"Tell you what," said Daisy. "If you go back to your tank now, I'll give you both a Cheesy Wotsit from my lunchbox when I get back."

"Oooh," said Furball, sounding interested. "What's a Wotsit?"

"I know—I know—I know—I know!"

squealed Burble excitedly. "They're them orange things that go crunch–crunch–crunch and then afterwards everything tastes of cheese. Even the air in your nose!"

"Woah," said Furball, "I have *got* to get me one of those."

"So we've got ourselves a deal then?" asked Daisy.

"Make it two," said Burble.

"Two what?" said Daisy.

"Two Wotsits each and you're on."

Daisy looked doubtful. "I don't want you to be sick," she said. "Two Wotsits seems an awful lot for one gerbil."

"We could save one for later," suggested Furball.

"Yeah *right*," said Burble. "That is *so* going to happen. But come on, two Wotsits won't kill us. What d'you say?"

Daisy nodded, took both little paws gently between finger and thumb and shook them.

"OK," she said. "Deal." Then, watching them scamper off towards the classroom, she remembered the register and quickly made her way towards the office.

As soon as school was over, Daisy grabbed her satchel and ran up the lane as fast as her legs would carry her. She could hardly wait to see Boom again, to tell him about the gerbils and ask him if there was anything special he wanted in his sandwich tomorrow.

But when she leant over the gate and called to him, there was no response.

Daisy was puzzled. Where was he? Boom always wandered out to see her when she called. Clambering over into the field, she made her way across to the old barn and peered through the broken window.

Apart from some straw and a rusty tractor, the barn was empty.

Boom was nowhere to be seen.

Ant Music

The next morning, Daisy woke up feeling sure
that Boom would be back in his usual place.
He had probably just gone out for a walk, she
thought. She decided to make him a treat and
was just putting an extra-thick ham and
ketchup sandwich into her lunchbox when her
dad came past on his way out to work.

"You must have hollow legs, Daisy," he
said, taking a quick swig of coffee and
ruffling her hair. "You've got enough in there
to feed an army!"

"She's a growing girl," said Mum. "Aren't you, love?"

"Hope so," said Daisy, who was still one of the smallest in her class.

"Now then," said Dad, kissing her on the top of her head. "Didn't I ever tell you that the best things come in small packages?"

Walking along the path next to the meadow, Daisy stopped and leant over the gate.

"Boom!" she called softly. "I've made your favourite sandwich!"

But there was still no sign of him.

And as Daisy listened, the only sound was the wind whispering softly past the stones and the grass and the broken window.

Miss Frink was so amazed to see Daisy arrive on time for once that she gave her a yellow smiley sticker and sent her up to the office with the register. The secretary was

busy, so Daisy sat on
a chair in the corridor
and thought about all
the unusual things
that had been
happening. And the
more she thought
about them, the
more ridiculous
they seemed.

A talking dog called Boom? Gerbils
discussing cheesy snacks? Swinging her feet
above the polished wooden floor, Daisy
watched specks of dust dancing in a shaft of
sunlight and decided that it was probably
time to stop daydreaming and join the real
world. Wasn't that what people were
always telling her? Maybe the sooner she
forgot about the whole thing, the better.

But even if Boom couldn't talk, she was
still worried about him. Where had he gone?

Daisy's thoughts were interrupted by a tiny sound, like someone singing a long way off.

"Dubbedy dum-dum, dee dubbedy, dubbedy dum-dum, dee dubbedy…"

She frowned. *What was that noise?*

"Dubbedy dum-dum, dee dubbedy, dubbedy dum-dum, dee dubbedy…"

Daisy jumped off her seat, got down on her hands and knees and peered beneath the chair. At first, all she could see was an old pen and a ball of fluff, but as she looked more closely she saw a tiny ant sitting in the dust, moving his head back and forth to the rhythm of the song.

So I wasn't imagining things, Daisy thought.

"Dubbedy dum-dum, dee dubbedy, dubbedy dum-dum, dee dubbedy…"

"Hello there, little ant," she said. "That's a nice song you're singing."

"Aaaaaaheee!"

The ant jumped up into the air and slowly backed away towards the skirting board.

"Don't be hurtin' me!" he said. "Don't be steppin' on me with them big shoesies!"

Daisy leant closer. "I'm not going to hurt you," she replied. "I was just enjoying your song."

The ant stopped.

"Really?" he asked. "Is you likin' me singin'?"

Daisy smiled.

"Yes, I is," she said.

"I is makin' it up meself," said the ant proudly. "Guess what it be called."

"I don't know," replied Daisy. "Dubbedy dum-dum?"

The ant was quiet for a moment.

"Lucky guess," he said at last.

Daisy sat back on her heels, stuck out her bottom lip and blew so that her fringe puffed up in the air. Today was turning out to be just as strange as yesterday.

"I is s'posed to be down in the Big Room where they's droppin' their biscuits," the ant explained. "Biscuits 'n' sugar."

"The staffroom you mean?" asked Daisy.

"Yus," said the ant. "There wus twenty of us in the patrol, see. I wus singin' an' dancin' an' enjoyin' meself and then the corporal says, 'Oi, Shorty, shuddup!' So then I sits down and starts to cry. And when I looks up again, they's all gone."

"Poor you," said Daisy
sympathetically.

"Yus," replied the ant. "Poor me is right, I
reckon."

"Why was the corporal cross with you?"

"He says ants who keeps singin' gets squashed by the big
shoesies. So now I'm doin' all me singin' under
the big chair. See?"

"I do see," said Daisy, trying
not to laugh. "Out the way of
the big shoesies, I suppose?"

"'Zactly," said the ant. "If you is squished by
the big shoesies, you can't sing no more and that is bad
and not happy. And," he added, "I likes bein' happy."

"Me too," agreed Daisy.

"You don't look happy, missus," said the ant.
"Is you scared of the big shoesies too?"

"No," said Daisy. "Big shoesies don't
really bother me. It's just…" She took a
deep breath. "Yesterday I was talking
to a dog, then I chatted to some gerbils,

and now I'm talking to an ant. And – I don't mean to be rude – but it's all a bit weird. So now I'm beginning to wonder if I might be dreaming."

"Oh no," said the ant. "If you was dreamin', you'd be snorkin'."

"Snorkin'?" Daisy asked. "What's that?"

"You know," said the ant. He lay down on his side, put two legs under his head and made little puffing noises. "Snorkin'."

"Oh, *snoring*," said Daisy. "Well yes, I suppose I would."

The ant scampered closer and looked up at her.

"Guess what, missus?"

"What?"

"I is not happy either."

"Oh dear," whispered Daisy. "Why not?"

"I *told* you," wailed the ant. "I is lost!"

"Lost?" said Daisy.

"Yus," said the ant. "Completerly and utterly."

"Well, perhaps I can help," offered Daisy. "I know where the staffroom is."

The ant shook his head. "No, no, I don't want biscuits no more. I is tired. I is wantin' to go home."

"Oh," said Daisy. "Well, which way is your nest?"

"If I was a-knowin' that," replied the ant, "me wouldn't be lost, would me?"

"I suppose not," agreed Daisy. "But how did you get here in the first place?"

"Marched," said the ant. "That's how ants is gettin' everywhere. Marchy–marchy–marchy, under the green wood-slab and over the brown shoesy-field."

Daisy thought for a moment. "Oh, you mean the front entrance," she said, remembering the green double doors at the end of the corridor. She guessed that the shoesy-field was probably the doormat where people wiped their feet. "I can take you there if you like. Climb up and I'll give you a ride."

Daisy stretched out her arm beneath the chair so that her hand was almost touching the ant. He took a few steps back and then slowly began to walk forwards again.

"Don't be squishin' me now," he said.

"Stop worrying," said Daisy. "I won't hurt you."

The ant touched the side of Daisy's finger with his tiny feelers and tickled his way along into the middle of her palm.

"Ready!" he said. "Off we goes!"

"OK," said Daisy. "Hold on tight."

She was about to pull her hand from beneath the chair when she heard footsteps and looked up to see Mr Blake, the headteacher, standing behind her.

"Ah, Daisy Dawson," he said. "What are you up to?"

Quick as a flash, Daisy folded her fingers over the top of the ant and jumped to her feet.

"Sorry, Mr Blake," she said. "I've just come to deliver the register."

"Hey!" called a little voice.

"What be goin' on?"

"*Shush!*" said Daisy.

"I beg your pardon?" said Mr Blake.

"Sorry," said Daisy. "I didn't mean you."

Mr Blake glanced around.

"Then who did you mean, exactly?"

"Who be there?"

"No one," said Daisy.

"Young lady," said Mr Blake, "do you make a habit of saying shush to no one?"

"Be it your corporal boss-man?"

"Yes," said Daisy. "Kind of." She glanced up and saw that Mr Blake was looking annoyed.

"I mean no!" she added hurriedly. "No, I don't make a habit of saying shush to no one." She wiped her forehead with the back of her hand. This was getting complicated.

"Well then," said Mr Blake, taking off his spectacles and polishing them with a cloth. "Perhaps you would like to explain."

"Daaaaai–zeeeee! Can I go back to me nest now, please? I wanna go a-sleepin' an' a-snorkin'. Daisy, Daisy, *Daaaaai-zeeeee!*"

"Would you please shut *up* for a minute?"

said Daisy crossly. Then she looked up at Mr Blake and blushed as she realized what she had just said.

Mr Blake glared at her so fiercely that her knees went wobbly.

"*What* did you say?" he demanded.

"Oh no, no, no – I didn't mean *you*, Mr Blake. I was, I was…" – Daisy thought desperately for a moment and was hit by a sudden flash of inspiration – "I was talking to my stomach!"

When he heard this, Mr Blake passed a hand over his eyes and shook his head.

"Your stomach?" he repeated wearily.

"Yes, Mr Blake. I don't think I had enough breakfast. It's been quite a morning."

"You is tellin' me, missus."

Daisy tried to ignore the fact that the ant was now doing a very energetic and tickly jig around the palm of her hand. Instead she did her best to look serious.

Mr Blake sighed. "Daisy, I really don't know what's got into you today, but I suggest that whatever it is, you let it out again as soon as possible."

"Yes, Mr Blake," said Daisy, trying hard not to giggle as the ant continued to boogie around inside her hand. "I shall certainly let it out as soon as I can."

Mr Blake took off his glasses again and waved her away with the back of his hand. "Go on then, child. Back to your classroom."

"See ya, Blakey Boy!" called the ant. "Careful with them shoesies!"

"You nearly got me in big trouble back there," said Daisy as she nipped out through the double doors into the playground.

"Nuffin' to do wiv me," said the ant. "I wus just dancin'."

"Hmm," said Daisy. "And interrupting."

50

"Yus," said the ant. "Dancin' and interruptin'. I is good at them things, isn't I, missus?"

"Tell me something," said Daisy. "Don't you think it's strange that we're talking to one another?"

"Nope," said the ant. "I is talkin' to anyone that be listenin'. Last week me talked to a caterpillar. That *wus* strange."

"Why?" asked Daisy.

"Well, we wus lookin' at the birds in the sky and he says, 'I'll be up there flying with 'em one day.' So I says, 'Yus right. Only if they eats you first!'"

"Actually, he was telling the truth," said Daisy. "Didn't you know? He'll turn into a butterfly next spring."

The ant laughed. "Me likes you," he said. "You is funny."

They reached the edge of the playing field and Daisy knelt down on the soft grass.

"There," she said. "Do you think you can find your way home now?"

"Oh, me house, me house!" cried the ant happily as Daisy opened her hand. "I is seein' me house!"

He walked to the end of Daisy's finger and stepped down onto a blade of grass. Then he turned round and waved his feelers at her.

"Thanks for the lift, Missus Daisy! Be seein' you again some day!"

"I hope so," said Daisy. She watched him crawl down the green stem to the brown earth below. "But how will I know it's you?"

"Easy," replied the ant.

"I is the one who be singin'!"

At that moment, a window opened and Daisy heard the familiar sound of Miss Frink's voice shouting at her from across the playground.

"Daisy Dawson," she yelled, "come back into the classroom this instant!"

"Uh-oh," said Daisy. "Got to go!"

But when she looked around, the ant had gone.

Daisy sat silently for a moment, breathing the scent of warm earth and listening to the murmur of the bees.

"Goodbye," she whispered. "Watch out for them shoesies!"

Then she jumped up and ran across the playground, hopping carefully over a small line of ants before disappearing through the double doors into the cool shadows of the corridor.

Sky-Flowers

As soon as school was over, Daisy
burst out through the front
doors and ran at top speed up
the lane.

Leaning on the gate, she rested her chin
on the top and called, "Boom, where are
you?"

When there was no reply, she cupped
her hands around her mouth and shouted,
"Boom, please! It's me – Daisy!"

"You're wasting your breath," said a husky voice beside her.

Daisy looked around to see a sleek grey cat staring up at her with cool green eyes.

"Boom's gone. Didn't you know?"

"But he can't have," said Daisy, who was already getting used to having conversations with animals. "I only spoke to him yesterday."

"Well yesterday was yesterday," replied the cat. "And today is today." It licked one of its paws, then looked up at Daisy again.

"The name's Trixie, by the way. Trixie McDixie if you want the whole of it, though there's not many that do."

She rubbed against the fence and padded closer.

"I warned him only the other day, but that dog always thinks he knows best. Well, not this time he doesn't."

"Trixie," said Daisy, "what are you talking about?"

"OK, listen up. Every morning at about eleven thirty, Boom goes into town to see the butcher's boy. He shows up, does his whiny dog thing and then the boy lobs a couple of scraggy bones at him. Can't see the attraction myself, but Boom says it's kind of a tradition and he never misses it. Until now, that is."

"Why?" asked Daisy. "What happened?"

"There's a new dog warden in town. Word on the street is that any dog without a tag is getting pulled in and thrown in the slammer. Boom just laughed when I told him about it. But he won't be laughing now. If no one claims him by the end of the week, they'll send him where they send all unwanted dogs."

"Where's that?" whispered Daisy.

"How should I know?" said Trixie. "All I know is, once a dog gets sent there, he never comes back."

"But that's terrible!" said Daisy. "We've got to do something!"

"Hmmm," purred Trixie. "Well let's see. Do you know where he's being kept? No. Could you get him out of there if you did? Probably not. So are you going to waste my time discussing it with me? Let's hope not."

"You don't seem to care very much," said Daisy, getting cross.

"I'm a cat," said Trixie. "Cats don't do drama."

"So that's it then?" asked Daisy. "You're just going to sit there and do nothing?"

"No," said Trixie calmly. "I'm going to say that if the daft dog had listened to me in the first place, he would never have got himself into this mess. Now if you'll excuse me," she added, strolling slowly towards the bushes, "I have a dinner date with a rabbit." And with that, she disappeared into the undergrowth.

The only sound was a gentle breeze rustling the leaves and, in the distance, a sparrow singing songs about rain.

Daisy stared after Trixie, shocked that she could be quite so unfeeling. Then she put her head against the gate and started to cry, the tears dripping down onto the cool green grass below.

"Hush now, my poppet," said a soft voice. "Nothing's as bad as all that."

Daisy lifted her head to find herself staring into the face of the white mare who lived in the field.

"Oh," she said, "hello." She dried her eyes with the back of her hand and felt the horse's

warm breath in her
hair. "Who are you?"

"My name's Meadowsweet,"
said the mare. "And you must be
Daisy Dawson."

"Yes," said Daisy, still sniffling. "How did
you know?"

"A yellow butterfly told me," replied
Meadowsweet. "She also told me that you
helped her when she was in trouble. So
now you should tell me why you're so sad
and maybe I can help you."

"It isn't me that needs help," said Daisy sadly. "It's Boom."

"Boom?" replied Meadowsweet, sounding surprised. "Why, what's he been up to?"

"Do you know him?" asked Daisy.

Meadowsweet stamped her foot and whinnied loudly. "Boom's lived here ever since he was born," she explained. "He's always been so kind and thoughtful, even as a puppy. When I got frightened by fireworks one evening, he told me to just think of them as sky-flowers and stayed up all night with me, making sure I was all right. I've never forgotten it. So what's happened?"

Daisy carefully recounted the story that Trixie had told her. When she finished, Meadowsweet leant over the gate and put her head against Daisy's cheek, so that her warm breath tickled Daisy's ear.

"Don't you listen to that old sourpuss," she whinnied. "Whatever happens, you and I will find a way to bring Boom home again."

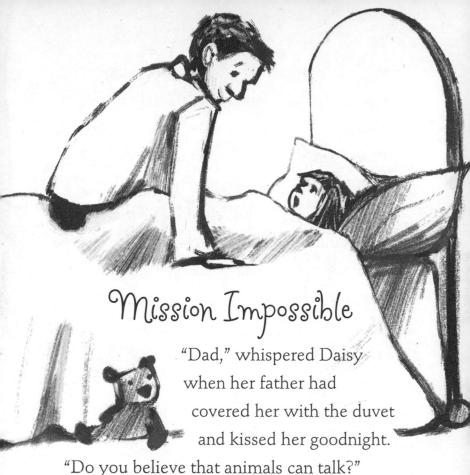

Mission Impossible

"Dad," whispered Daisy when her father had covered her with the duvet and kissed her goodnight. "Do you believe that animals can talk?"

He stopped in the doorway and turned back to look at her.

"Of course," he said.

"Really?" asked Daisy.

"Yes, I'm sure they can – at least in their own way. Otherwise, how would rabbits warn each other that a fox was coming? Or a bee tell its friends about a field full of flowers?"

"Oh," said Daisy. "I hadn't thought of that."

"Of course," her father went on, "the really interesting thing would be if we could understand what they were saying." He chuckled. "That would be something, wouldn't it?"

"Yes," Daisy whispered as he turned out the light. "It certainly would."

At first, she wasn't sure what had woken her. The moonlight traced silver patterns across the floorboards, and as she rubbed her eyes, Daisy heard a faint tap-tap-tapping at the window. Cautiously she pulled back the curtains and was surprised to see a little grey squirrel sitting on the ledge. It waved when it saw her and pointed at the window catch.

66

Daisy quickly opened the window and
the squirrel jumped down onto her bed.

"Greetings," it said in a small, posh voice.
"I am here on a top secret mission." It
beckoned her closer, put a paw up to its
mouth and whispered, "No one must ever
know of my existence."

"How exciting," said Daisy, trying to look
serious. "Are you a spy?"

"Maybe I am," replied the squirrel, "and
maybe I'm not."

He looked slowly left and right as though checking that no one was listening, then whispered, "The blue donkey ... is under the mattress."

Daisy leant over the side of her bed and peered beneath it. "Really?" she asked. "Are you sure?"

"No, no, no, *no!*" replied the squirrel, exasperation creeping into his voice. He cupped both paws around his mouth and said again in a loud whisper, "THE BLUE DONKEY IS UNDER THE MATTRESS!"

Daisy shook her head. "I'm sorry, but I haven't got the faintest idea what you're talking about."

He dropped his paws and sighed heavily.

"It's secret code!" he explained. "Trouble is, I'm the only one who understands it."

"Never mind," said Daisy brightly. "How about you tell me in ordinary language?"

"OK," he said. "We've found Boom. We know where he is."

"Oh," gasped Daisy, picking him up and kissing him on the tip of the nose. "That's wonderful news, Mr Squirrel!"

"Oh, well now, it was nothing really. I–I – please, call me Cyril," he said, blushing in a way that only squirrels can.

"Cyril?" asked Daisy, placing him gently back down onto the duvet. "Cyril the Squirrel?"

"Yes," he replied. "Blame my mother. Lovely lady, but partial to a rhyme."

"So tell me," Daisy went on, "where did you find Boom?"

"Well, that's the problem," said Cyril. "At the moment he's locked up in temporary kennels on the outskirts of town, run by some crazy lady, apparently. But they're going to move him to the big city kennels in the morning. And once they've done that,

we won't have a hope of rescuing him."
Cyril's voice dropped. "We have to get
him out *tonight*."

"Tonight?" whispered Daisy excitedly.
"But how?"

"Well," said the squirrel, eyeing
Daisy's pyjamas disdainfully, "getting
dressed would be a start."

A few minutes later, Daisy
clicked the front door
shut behind her and
followed Cyril down
the driveway. As they
turned the corner, she
saw Meadowsweet
waiting beneath a
streetlamp.

"Well done, Cyril," said the old mare, bending her head down towards Daisy. "Climb aboard, Daisy. We must move quickly."

Daisy clambered up onto Meadowsweet's back, the moon shining silver above the chimney pots. Cyril scrambled up onto her shoulder and then they were off, the squirrel calling out directions as they galloped away across moonlit fields, the cool night air blowing softly in their faces.

After about twenty minutes they came to a white farmhouse on the edge of a wood. Behind it was a high wooden fence with a sign that said:

```
KRACKDOWN KENNELS
     KEEP OUT
```

"Are you sure this is it?" asked Daisy.

"Absolutely," said Cyril. "I got a couple of pigeons and some mice to case the joint this afternoon. Cost me a few acorns, but if you want good information, you've got to pay for it these days."

"We think Boom's the only one in there at the moment," explained Meadowsweet. "The other dogs were moved out last week."

"OK," said Cyril, perching on Meadowsweet's head. "Here's the plan. On the other side of that fence is a row of metal cages. Boom's kennel is inside cage number seven. But the cages are locked and the keys are kept by the fierce old bat who owns the place."

"Where does she keep them?" asked Daisy.

"On her bedside table," replied Cyril.

Daisy chewed her lip. "That's not so good."

"Ah, but that's where you come in," he explained. "I nip through the catflap and unlatch the door, you come upstairs and open the bedroom door for me, and I sneak in and swipe the keys. We'll be in and out before she's even got time to grab her baseball bat."

"Baseball bat?" repeated Daisy nervously. "Did you say baseball bat?"

"Don't worry," said Cyril. "She couldn't hit a home run if you bowled her a water melon."

Daisy took a deep breath. "OK then. I suppose we'd better get on with it."

"That's the spirit," said Cyril, leaping up onto the fence. "Who dares wins!"

As he disappeared over the top, Daisy stood on Meadowsweet's back, hooked her fingers over the fence and pulled herself up. She jumped down, nearly squashing Cyril flat. He rolled out of the way just in time. "Hey!" he squeaked. "I'm on your side, remember?"

The house was in darkness as they approached, and Cyril slipped quietly through the catflap. A few seconds later he reappeared with a key in his mouth and Daisy quickly opened the front door.

Standing in the darkness at the bottom of the stairs, she felt her fingers tingle with a mixture of excitement and fear.

"Come on," said Cyril, scampering upstairs towards the bedroom.

The house smelled of old carpets and decaying flowers. Daisy stopped and held her breath every time a stair creaked, but at last she reached the bedroom door, where Cyril was tapping his foot and beckoning impatiently to her.

"This is it," he whispered. "You open the door, I'll grab the keys and then *whoosh!* we're *out* of here."

"OK," Daisy whispered back. "But be careful."

She twisted the doorknob and the door creaked open. Over on the bed, a large mound rose and fell beneath the duvet, accompanied by loud snores and wheezes.

"Look," said Cyril. "What d'you reckon?"

Daisy followed his gaze to the bedside table and, trying to ignore the baseball bat propped up against it, saw a small lamp, a glass of water and a bunch of keys.

"Bingo," she whispered. "Go for it, Cyril!"

Cyril ran around the end of the bed and jumped neatly up onto the table.

Unfortunately for him, the table top had been waxed and polished that very morning and now it was as slippery as an ice rink. Daisy saw the look of horror on his face as he pirouetted unsteadily across the surface before colliding with the table lamp and knocking the glass to the floor with a crash.

For a few short
moments, time seemed to stand still. Then a
large, ruddy-faced woman rose up from the
duvet and began to scream so loudly that
Daisy jumped backwards and bumped her
head against the doorframe.

"It's a rat!" screeched the woman, pointing
a thick, stubby finger at Cyril as he stood
transfixed among the wreckage of the table
top. "I'm being attacked by a filthy rat!"

As she sprang out of bed with a heavy
thud, Cyril came to his senses and shot out

of the bedroom like a
stone from a catapult.

"Leg it, Daisy!" he squeaked,
rocketing past. "She's after us!"

Daisy turned and began leaping down the
stairs three at a time.

"Did you hear that?" yelled Cyril as they
burst through the back door and ran
towards the kennels. "She called me a *rat*!"

"Never mind that," said Daisy. They
skidded to a halt in front of cage number
seven. "Where are the keys?"

Cyril looked at her awkwardly.

"I–I … might have, err, dropped them at
the top of the stairs," he said. "I sort of …
didn't want to get clobbered."

"Brilliant," said Daisy.

They looked round to see the
kennel owner standing at the back
door, brandishing the
baseball bat above her
head. "Where are you,
you sneaky rat?" she
shrieked. "Come on out
or I'll whack you with
my walloper!"
"Quick, Cyril,"
urged Daisy,
crouching next to the
kennels, "what's plan B?"
She put her hand against
the wire of the cage to
steady herself, but the
door swung open and
she fell forward onto her hands and knees.
"Cyril!" she whispered. "Look, it's open!"
Cyril squeaked in surprise and
disappeared into the cage. Daisy glanced

back to see the large figure of the kennel owner walking slowly across the grass towards them, clutching the baseball bat firmly in her right hand.

"Cyril," Daisy called nervously, "she's coming!"

The squirrel emerged from the gloom shaking his head. "This is not going quite as planned," he whispered. "There's no sign of him."

"Hey, you there!" shouted the woman. "Girl with the rat!"

Cyril looked up at Daisy with a pained expression.

"What *is* it with this rat thing?" he asked.

"Cyril," said Daisy, "she looks pretty angry. What are we going to do?"

Cyril watched calmly as the woman stomped towards them. "Emergency tactics," he said. "I'll create a diversion and you make a break for it over the fence."

"But she might whack you," Daisy protested, cowering back against the cage. "With her walloper!"

"You forget," said Cyril loftily, "that she is a mere civilian, whereas *I* am a highly trained squirrel operative. The poor woman doesn't stand a *chance*." And before Daisy had time to answer, he ran off at top speed across the grass.

There was a sudden swishing noise and Cyril leapt high into the air with a cry of "Hiiiiii-*yah!*", holding his paws like a tiny Ninja warrior as the baseball bat swept harmlessly beneath him. Eyes narrowed, he made small, high-pitched squeaks, jumping deftly out of the way as the hapless kennel owner took more swipes at him. "Go, Daisy," he shouted. "Run for it!"

But as Daisy reached the fence, a booming voice stopped her in her tracks.

"And where do you think you're going?" The red-faced woman was marching straight towards her. "You stay right where you are, young lady!"

Stretching up on tiptoe, Daisy tried desperately to reach the top of the fence, but it was too high. Her fingers scrabbled uselessly against the wood as two strong hands grabbed her arms.

"Ha-*ha!*" cried the woman triumphantly. "Now I've got you."

Shaking with fear, Daisy leant her forehead against the fence and called, "Meadowsweet, help me, please!"

The next moment there was a thundering of hooves and Meadowsweet sailed over the fence to land beside Daisy with an earth-shaking thump. The woman's mouth fell open in amazement and she sank to the ground with her hands clamped firmly over her eyes.

"It's a bad dream, Beatrice," she mumbled to herself, shaking her head and rubbing her eyes. "You're having a bad dream, that's all. Dancing rats and flying horses, indeed! Just count up to ten and it'll all be over. One, two…"

Meadowsweet tossed her mane, called, "Climb aboard, brave soldiers," and before Daisy knew it they had leapt back over the fence and were galloping away through silent woods and moonlit fields towards home.

*　*　*

As Daisy opened the gate to let Meadowsweet into her field, she saw that Cyril looked sad and angry with himself.

"Mission most definitely *not* accomplished," he said miserably. "Now we'll never see Boom again."

"It's not your fault, Cyril," said Daisy. "You did everything you could."

"But it wasn't enough, was it?" Cyril cried bitterly. "It wasn't *enough*!"

"Oh puh–*lease*," said a sharp voice from somewhere in the shadows, "I've already had enough of that dog whining all night. Don't make me listen to the squirrel as well."

Peering into the darkness, Daisy could see the green eyes of Trixie McDixie staring at them from beneath the horse trough.

"For your information," replied Cyril icily, "*that dog*, as you call him, has been taken away from us for ever. But I don't suppose you care about that, do you? I bet you're not even the slightest bit worried."

"You're right," said Trixie, carelessly licking her paw with her little pink tongue. "I'm not worried at all."

"Trixie!" Meadowsweet scolded. "You should be ashamed of yourself."

The cat stopped for a moment and twitched her whiskers in surprise.

"Oh," she said. "Do you really think so?" Then she padded out from beneath the horse trough and called huskily, "What about you, Boom? Do you think I should be ashamed of myself?"

Cyril frowned and looked at Daisy.

Daisy looked at Meadowsweet.

All three of them stared at the old barn.

Slowly, a large bloodhound emerged with the somewhat bewildered look of a dog

who is still half-asleep. Daisy flung her arms
around his neck and cried, "Oh Boom,
you're safe, you're safe!"

"Well, *duh!*" said Trixie.

Meadowsweet stamped and whinnied
with joy; but Cyril was flummoxed.

"I don't get it," he said. "The mice told me
the keys were in the bedroom. I even picked
them up. So how did Boom escape?"

"That," replied Trixie disdainfully, "is the trouble with mice. They may taste good, but they know nothing about modern security systems." She pushed a small rectangle of plastic towards Cyril, who sniffed it and shrugged.

"What's this?"

"This, my friend, is the key to the new electronic locks the kennel owner had fitted last week. The old keys you picked up were completely useless. I got chatting to the tomcat who lives there and he told me about this swipecard which opens all the kennels. So while she was out shopping this afternoon, I slipped in through the catflap, took the card off the table and gave the daft dog his freedom back."

"But how did you get him over the fence?" asked Cyril.

"No need," said Trixie. "Royston Rabbit owed me a favour or two, so after dinner last night I got him and his boys to dig a bit of a hole around the back. Nothing fancy, mind you – just big enough to let an old hound squeeze through."

Cyril stared at Trixie for a long time and then shook his head in disbelief.

"Do you mean to tell me," he said, "that while we were out there *risking our lives* this evening, you and Boom were back here relaxing?"

"Well, I wouldn't exactly call it relaxing," replied Trixie. "That dog snores like a sick horse."

Screwing his paws up into angry little fists, Cyril jumped up and down and squeaked, "Why on EARTH didn't you tell us before?"

Trixie shrugged. "Because, my dear squirrel, you never asked."

Cyril stamped his foot, scowled
furiously and scampered up a nearby
tree trunk in a major huff.

"Well," said Meadowsweet, as Daisy
hugged Boom, and Cyril sat sulking on a
branch of the old oak, "I have to say, Trixie,
you certainly showed us the way to do it
this time."

Trixie stared coolly at Meadowsweet for
a long moment, her eyes glowing green in
the moonlight.

"So what's new?" she purred.

And with that, she turned her back and
slunk off into the shadows.

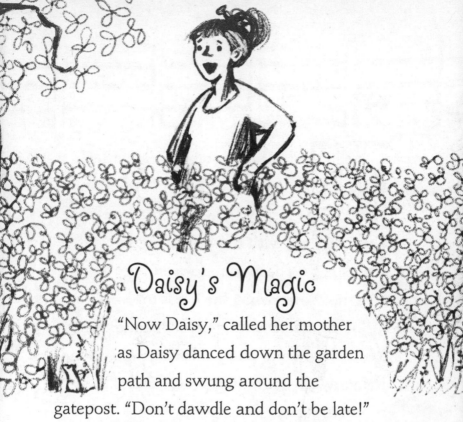

Daisy's Magic

"Now Daisy," called her mother
as Daisy danced down the garden
path and swung around the
gatepost. "Don't dawdle and don't be late!"

The sun shone brightly from a cloudless
sky, and somewhere among the green
leaves, a blackbird sang a song about
buttercups and rainbows.

"Don't worry, Mum," Daisy called back
over her shoulder, "Daisy Dawson is on
her way!"

She looked at her watch and saw that
there was still plenty of time before school
started. The family had spent the weekend
away staying with her grandparents, and
now she was desperate to see Boom again
and show him what she'd got for him.

She crossed the road carefully and ran up
the path towards the field where she found
Meadowsweet grazing peacefully in the
morning sun.

"Hello, Meadowsweet!" said Daisy
happily. "Where is everyone this morning?"

Meadowsweet shook her head and
snorted. Then she bent down and began
tugging at the grass again.

"Hey, Meadowsweet," said Daisy. "Aren't
you talking to me today?"

"She ain't called Meadowsweet," said
a voice behind her. "She's called Dobbin."

Daisy turned around to see the farmer
coming up the lane. "Reckon you should be
in school learning summat useful, young 'un,"
he said as he passed. "Not wastin' your time
talkin' to dumb animals."

As Daisy watched the grumpy old farmer
walk away up the path, she suddenly felt
completely alone, as though the ground had
opened up and swallowed everything she'd
ever believed in.

It's time to wake up… whispered the voice in her head … *they were only dreams … none of it was real … they were only dreams…*

In the silence that followed, Daisy blinked back tears and felt her happiness evaporate like morning mist. For the first time in her life, she began to suspect that the things people said about her were true. That she spent too much time living in imaginary worlds that didn't really exist. Suddenly it was obvious to her, as clear as the sunlight that shone through the trees.

Her adventures with the animals had been dreams; nothing more. Meadowsweet was just a horse called Dobbin, and everyone knew that horses couldn't talk.

And so, as Daisy began to wander back along the path towards school, she decided that the time had come to stop believing in her dreams. It was time to grow up and join the real world.

From now on, she would listen.

She would be good.

She would be on time…

"Hey, poppet," called a familiar voice. "Going so soon?"

Daisy stopped and frowned. Then she shook her head and began walking again.

Stop it, she told herself. *Grow up!*

"Daisy, my love!" called the voice behind her. "Where are you going?"

Daisy turned and saw that the white mare was leaning over the gate, staring at her.

"Meadowsweet?" she asked, hardly daring to hope.

The mare nodded. "Yes of course, dear. Who did you think it was?"

Daisy was confused. "But … when I spoke to you just now … you didn't answer."

"Well of course not, my lovely," replied Meadowsweet. "I could hardly have a chat with you while that silly old farmer was standing there, could I? *Dobbin* indeed!"

Daisy suddenly felt as though her heart was going to burst. She ran back up the path, flung her arms around Meadowsweet's nose and kissed her.

"Well now," said Meadowsweet, her breath warm in Daisy's ear. "That's more like my Daisy."

Then she glanced over Daisy's shoulder and said, "Look. There's someone else to see you."

When Daisy turned around, she saw that Boom was sitting in the lane, gazing up at her with his serious brown eyes.

"Boom!" she cried.

"Hello, Daisy," he said in a voice that was deep and slow and kind. "I woke up early this morning and thought, I wonder if my favourite little girl would like some company on her way to school?"

Daisy smiled and thought that she had never been so happy in all her life.

"That would be just lovely," she said. "But before we go, I have something for you."

"For me?" asked Boom. Then after a moment's thought he added, "Has it got ham in it?"

"No," said Daisy, reaching into her satchel, "but I think you'll like it anyway." She pulled out a small tag on a silver chain and held it up for Boom to see.

"What is it?" he asked.

"It's a name tag," said Daisy, kneeling down and fastening the chain around his neck. "It's got your name on the front and my name and telephone number on the back. If the dog warden ever sees you again, he'll think you belong to me and he'll leave you alone."

Boom looked up at Daisy.

"Do I?" he asked shyly.

"Do you what, Boom?"

"Do I belong to you?"

Daisy put her arms around him.

"Friends belong to one another," she said.
"Isn't that right, Meadowsweet?"

Meadowsweet nodded. "It's the best sort
of belonging there is."

Boom rested his chin contentedly in
Daisy's lap and for a few moments all was
silent except for the gentle humming of the
bees. Then suddenly he pricked up his ears
and barked twice.

"What is it, Boom?" Daisy asked, stroking
his head. "What's the matter?"

"Oh, nothing really. I just think we ought
to be going, that's all."

"But why?" asked Daisy.

"Because," said Boom, "the school bell is ringing."

"Uh-oh," said Daisy. "I'm going to be late again, aren't I?" She stuck her bottom lip out and blew so that her fringe puffed up in the air. "Meadowsweet, do you mind if I ask you something before I go?"

"Not at all," said Meadowsweet. "Ask me anything."

"Do you think I'll always be able to talk to you all? Or do you think it's some kind of magic that might disappear one day?"

"I don't know," said Meadowsweet gently. "But what I do know is that whenever we talk, the magic seems to come from inside of you. It's part of who you are, Daisy Dawson, and that is a very rare thing. You must always look after it, and keep it close to your heart."

"Thank you, Meadowsweet," said Daisy, kissing the old mare lightly on the nose. "I'll try."

Then she hitched up her satchel and
ran away down the hot, dusty lane towards
the gates of Nettlegreen Primary School,
with her best friend Boom by her side.

A TiNY BEACH...
AN UPTURNED BOAT...
A WHiSPER OF SMOKE...

When Flotsam and Jetsam are washed
ashore, they soon become the best of
friends. Every day brings a new adventure.
Join them as they battle a spiteful seagull,
build a new home and rescue a very shy
hermit crab.

A FLASH OF LIGHTNING.
A ROAR OF THUNDER
A PIERCING CRY...

Flotsam and Jetsam live on a tiny beach.
One night a great storm brings them
a surprise – a huge heap of bedraggled
feathers that turns out to be more trouble
than they thought...

BEL MOONEY

Big Dog

Bonnie

The little dog with big ideas

"That's not a dog Mum — not a PROPER dog!"

The dog in Harry's dreams is big, strong, brown-and-black-mixed. The dog in Harry's kitchen is tiny, white and fluffy, and looks like a rabbit. To make matters worse, his mum has named her *Bonnie*.

But Bonnie has her own ideas. Can she show Harry that big things sometimes come in small fluffy parcels?

Steve Voake is the author of two novels, *The Dreamwalker's Child* and *The Web of Fire*. *Daisy Dawson* is his first book for younger readers. Before becoming a full-time writer, he was headteacher of the "Jack and Jill" school in Kilmersdon, Somerset, which has the original well from the nursery rhyme in its playground at the top of the hill. Steve lives in Somerset.

Jessica Meserve illustrates and designs books for children. She is the author/illustrator of the picture book *Small*, and has illustrated several other titles including *Drawing Together* by Mimi Thebo and *Grandad and John* by Jeanne Willis. Jessica lives in Edmonton, Canada, where she passes the long winters drawing, making pots and practising yoga.